My Teacher's My Friend

Written and Illustrated
by

P.K. Hallinan

For
Arlene Johnston, Luey Huggins,
Susan Graybill & Bobbi Roberts
and
other dedicated teachers
everywhere.

Ideals Children's Books • Nashville, Tennessee
an imprint of Hambleton-Hill Publishing, Inc.

Copyright © 1989 by Patrick K. Hallinan
Published by Ideals Children's Books
An imprint of Hambleton-Hill Publishing, Inc.
Nashville, Tennessee 37218
All rights reserved.
Printed and bound in the United States of America

ISBN 0-8249-8542-7 (pbk.)
ISBN 1-57102-155-8 (hc)

My teacher's my friend,
and I guess you could say
I've got all kinds of reasons
for feeling this way.

She greets us each morning
on the playing field grass.

She helps us line up
and march into class.

The next thing we know,
we're singing a song
while our teacher chimes in
and sings right along.

We pledge our allegiance
with our hands on our hearts.

We dance all around
just to loosen our parts.

Once she's called roll
to find out who's there,
our teacher pulls up
her storybook chair.

And nobody tells
a story so well.

But then it's our busy bee
time of the day
when everyone goes
their own separate way.

And each of us has
a job we must do,
like "Lights-and-Door Helper"...

and "Paper Helper" too!

So we march all around
in an organized spin
till everyone's ready
for the work to begin.

We paint pictures with sponges
of all different shapes.

We make clever posters
with scissors and tape.

We even dress up
in the funniest ways
to discuss big events
and observe special days.

Then all of us honor
the "Star of the Week"
as one of us gets up
to share and to speak.

And one thing we've learned
is we all get a turn.

She shows us a movie
every once in a while.

She brings in guest speakers
to share things worthwhile.

She even takes care
when somebody cries
to smooth out their problems
and help dry their eyes.

My teacher's amazing,
I have to admit.
She helps us to spell.

She helps us stay fit.

And when the day's done,
without any fuss
she guides us outside
to find the right bus.

Yes, she's there when we need her,
from beginning to end.

My teacher's my leader...

My teacher's my friend.